CARMAN PRESENTS

NO MONSTERS

A Storybook for Kids

ALBURY PUBLISHING

Carman Presents No Monsters
A Storybook for Kids
ISBN 1-88008-935-1
Copyright © 1996 by Carman Ministries
P.O. Box 5093
Brentwood, TN 37024-5093

Published by ALBURY PUBLISHING
P.O. Box 470406
Tulsa, OK 74147-0406

Hey Kids!

Here's a new book about a story that could really help you out. It's called, *NO MONSTERS*. So pay attention, and get ready to learn — how to MONSTER-PROOF your life!

I took authority
in Christ. All fear
flew away.
I stood bold as
a lion and ran it
off when it heard
me say—

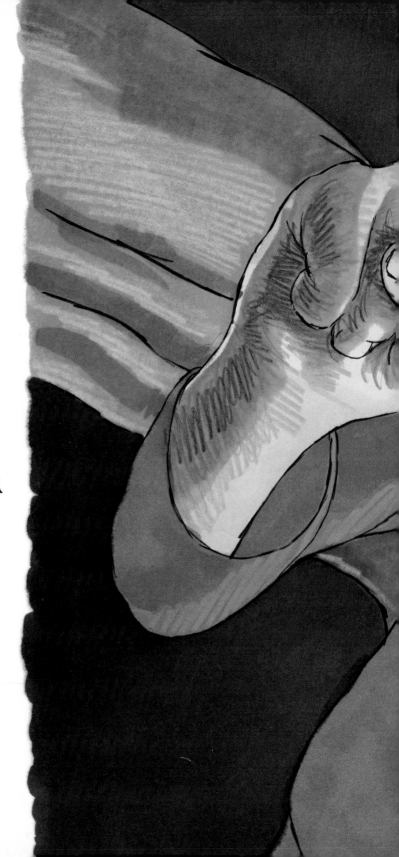

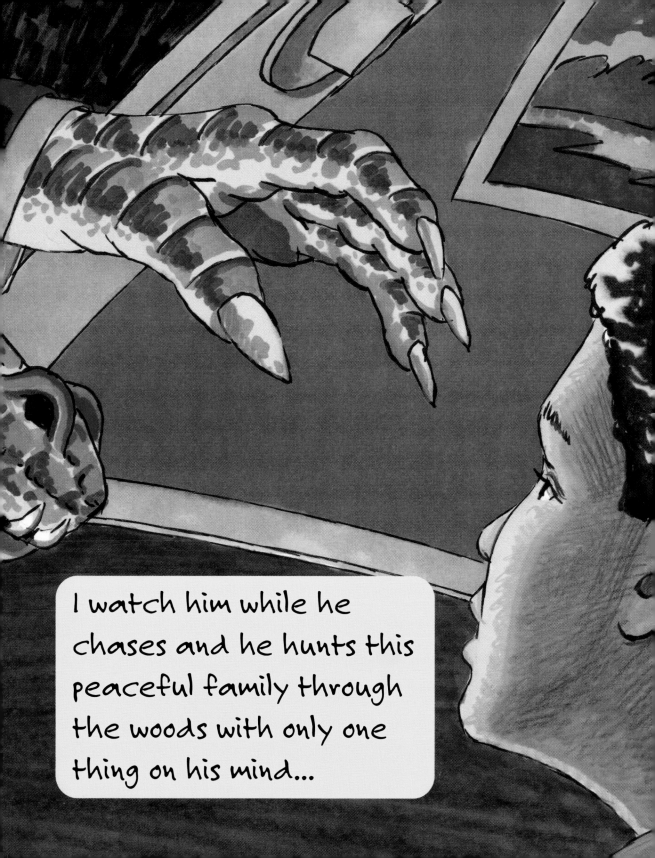

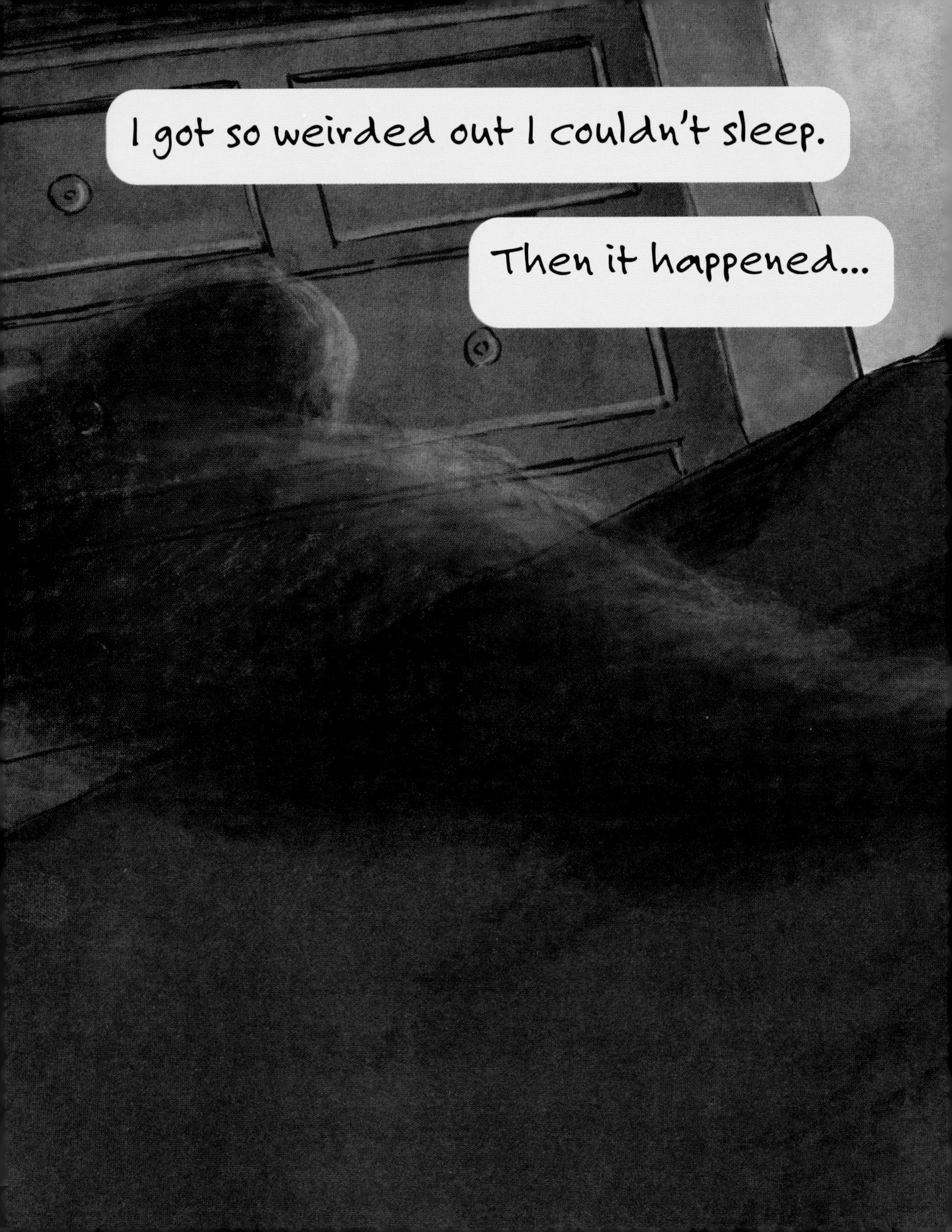
I got so weirded out I couldn't sleep.
Then it happened...

...an evil spirit floated by my bed.

I got righteously indignant! I was gonna make that demon pay! I could hardly believe the nerve of this little punk demon.
I thought, Heyyyy...all right! That's it, you're dead!

The anointing came upon me. I chased it out when it heard me say...

Watching horror movies on television can bring on a spirit of fear and bring creepy monster nightmares into your life. And that's not cool. If this happens to you, you need to MONSTER-PROOF YOUR LIFE! You need to "...fix your thoughts on what is true and good and right..." (TLB). That's what the apostle Paul tells us to do in Philippians 4:8 — whether it's daytime — or whether it's night.

Remember to speak the name of Jesus Christ whenever Satan's little punk demons try to keep you awake at night. Get righteously indignant! Take authority in Christ!

Never forget there is power in Jesus' blood. The Bible says we overpower the devil's evil through the word of our testimony and the work of Christ's blood (Revelation 12:11).

So if an evil spirit tries to visit your house tonight, get up like I did, and say — I AM THE TEMPLE OF THE HOLY GHOST, AND I'M PROTECTED BY THE LORD OF HOSTS! GET OUT! IN THE NAME OF JESUS CHRIST. 'CAUSE I DON'T WANT NO MONSTERS IN MY HOUSE TONIGHT!

No Monsters Bible Truths

When young Carman laid wide awake that night, the shadow that moved wasn't real. It was his imagination that had been stirred up by a spirit of fear because of watching that scary movie. When the evil spirit floated by his bed, it was only a lying spirit of fear.

The Bible tells us in 2 Corinthians 10:5 to "Cast down imaginations, and every high thing that exalts itself against the knowledge of God," so we can, "bring into captivity every thought to the obedience of Christ" (KJV). We do this by reading God's Word and by praying to Him. When we do these things, the spirit of fear that was bothering young Carman can't keep us awake. Why? Because the Bible tells us in 2 Timothy 1:7 that, "God did not give us a spirit that makes us afraid. He gave us a spirit of power and love and self-control" (ICB). We know this for sure when we pray and fellowship with Jesus in His Word. Then we can be bold as a lion because Proverbs 28:1 says, "The righteous are bold as a lion" (KJV)!

Carman could rebuke those lying spirits of fear that tried to scare him because of the authority Christ gave him. Jesus gave all His followers authority to rebuke demons in Luke 10:17-19. Listen to what Jesus' disciples said to Him after they received this authority: "Even the demons obey us when we use your name." Now listen to what Jesus told them! "I saw Satan falling from heaven as a flash of lightning! And I have given you authority over all the power of the Enemy, and to walk among serpents and scorpions [which Jesus referred to as demons], and to crush them. Nothing shall injure you" (TLB)!

When we use Jesus' name and speak His Word, demons have to flee! "And those who believe shall use my authority to cast out demons..." (Mark 16:17) [TLB]. This was true for Carman, and this is true for you! Demons have to flee in Jesus' name!

Additional copies of this book are available
from your local bookstore.

Albury Publishing
P.O. Box 470406, Tulsa, OK 74147

Other books available through Albury Publishing form Carman Ministries
R.I.O.T. Devotional Volume 1
R.I.O.T. Devotional Volume 2
Satan, Bite The Dust! A Storybook for Kids
Don't Quit! by Joseph S. Jones
Fatal Affliction by Joseph S. Jones

Available at your local bookstore.

MINISTRIES

Just 4 Kidz Product Order Form

ALL PRICES ARE IN U.S. DOLLARS

MUSIC
Cassettes - $10   CDs - $15

Yo Kidz!. . . . . _____   _____
Lawrence & The B. Attitudes . . . . _____   _____
Yo Kidz! 2 . . . . _____   _____

VIDEOS ($20 ea.)
Carman Yo Kidz! . . . . _____

NEW — CHILDREN'S BOOKS — Carman Presents:
1. Satan Bite The Dust ($10) . . . . _____
2. No Monsters ($10) . . . . _____
3. Who's In The House ($10). . . . . _____
4. There Is A God ($10). . . . . _____

TO ORDER

QTY.	ITEM	PRICE	TOTAL

Carman Ministries
Partner Number:

__ __ __ __ __ __ D

	U.S. Shipping/Handling	$6.00
	Outside U.S. Shipping/Handling	$20.00
	TOTAL AMOUNT DUE	

Name: _____

Address: _____
CANNOT SHIP TO POST OFFICE BOX

City:_____ State: _____ Zip: _____

Phone: _____
Allow 2-4 weeks delivery

Payment Type: ❑ Check ❑ Money Order ❑ VISA ❑ MasterCard ❑ Discover ❑ American Express

Credit Card #: _____ Exp. Date: _____

Name on Credit Card: _____

ALL OFFERS ARE GOOD WHILE SUPPLIES LAST.

PRODUCT DEPARTMENT c/o Carman Ministries
P.O. Box 5093 • Brentwood, TN 37024-5093(615) 371-1528 Fax (615) 371-5128